B.E.N. (PART 2)

THE SUCCESSFUL FAILURE

SOURADIP GHOSH

I dedicate this book to my grandmother LATE PROBHA GHOSH whose love and insane belief upon me gave me the motivation to bring my thoughts into paper.

I never say 'Wish you were here' because I know that 'You are and will always be with me'.....

LOVE YOU DIDA !!!

Contents

Preface

Every crime has a motive and to find out the criminal , one must detect the motive at the outset. But what if the motive is missing ?

After their first success , B.E.N. is now called upon to investigate upon a crime with no apparent motive. Investigations and interrogations seems to complicate the already jumbled up case. B.E.N. is also aware that if they fail to solve the case, their first success will be treated as their good luck and their efforts and sweats will all go to vain.

Will B.E.N. be able to solve the case ?

The answer is in the pages of the second installment of the B.E.N. series. So read on and enjoy the thrilling ride of spinechilling revelations and mind bending twists.

Prologue

It was an early Sunday morning when Mrs. Laxmi Devi, like every other day, had just finished her daily after bath worship of Lord Shiva. After worship, she was walking all over her house as a part of her regular routine with the plate of fresh flowers, sweets and burning candle spreading the purity of the mixed fragrance to every corner possible.

Suddenly someone slapped her very hard from her back and the plate flew away from her hand and landed onto the concrete floor with a bang. She also fell down and the attack happened so suddenly that she barely got any chance to react.

Before she could have understood the situation and shouted for help, a pair of booted legs kicked her with a huge force onto her belly. The pain was so much excruciating that though she shouted at her highest possible decibel; no sound came out of her voice.

The attacker kicked her for four more times at the same place on her belly with a force each greater than the previous one. Then the pair of legs changed its position and walking two steps left, kicked with full force on her face. The spectacles that she was wearing broke and a part of the glass got inserted into her right eye.

The attacker again kicked targeting her nose breaking it and making a pool of blood draining out of it. Then the attacker grabbed her by her hair and started dragging her like some carcass all over the house.

Mrs. Laxmi Devi was already half unconscious by then ----------- only conscious enough to feel the unbearable last few moments of pain that she was undergoing. She didn't know what was paining her more ------------- belly, eye, nose or her skull.

Finally after dragging her all over her house, the attacker took her to the kitchen, turned on the gas and put her face inside the burning flame.

CHAPTER ONE

FEELINGS

After solving the Malpani case, Bornali, Ellias and Nakul became quite famous. Columns were written about them in the newspapers and press interviews were held by media houses making their faces known among the throng.

Now when they walk in the crowd, people recognize them. Unknown people come and talk to them, asks them to take photograph with them, some even asks them their contact numbers. At the outset, they felt nervous, scared and embarrassed but now they have learned to enjoy the fame.

Unintentionally, a rapport has also been created between them and the police department, thanks to Mr. Sunirmol Ghoshal, who was the primarily involved officer in the Malpani case.

It was 4:30 PM in the evening when Nakul was sitting at his place reading a book. The main door opens and Bornali walks in. She takes off her shades and then closes the door. She had recently colored her hair and though she closed the door, sunrays were entering through the windows and as they were touching her hairs, it seemed burgundy.

She walked towards Nakul and took her seat in the chair adjacent to the sofa where Nakul was sitting.

Bornali was looking troubled and her expression was such as if she was expecting as to when Nakul will be asking her *what's up?*

When Nakul did not begin the conversation but just kept staring at her waiting for her to begin the conversation, she unwillingly had to break the ice.

"You should really talk to Ellias" were the first words that came out of her.

"Why? What happened?" asked Nakul putting down the book and after a small pause added, "now"

Bornali took a deep breath and then said carrying a lot of disgust in her communication, "Yesterday, he took me to a romantic candle light dinner at Taj and then talked all the cliché romantic lines we have heard a million of times in movies and read about in novels and then when I realized that he was thinking of proposing me there in front of all those strangers to be his girlfriend, I took off by lying that I am not feeling well."

Nakul listened to her with absolute calmness in his eyes as he was not at all surprised by Ellias's actions.

"I can't lie to him every time, you know" she said getting a bit agitated and then added, "So I was just wishing that if you could talk with him so that I don't have to break his heart."

"What is there to talk about? I thought you loved him" said Nakul with absolute honesty.

"I still love him Nakul" confessed Bornali without any hesitation and then continued, "But the feelings that he has for me is not love. It's called infatuation."

"How are you so sure that it's infatuation instead of love?" asked Nakul and then added, "May be he genuinely loves you and you are just shying away from the truth."

"I am not shying away from anything" said Bornali lividly "It's Ellias we are here talking about. He might be 24 but he hasn't crossed the mental age of 18 yet and you know that very well. We have already talked about it"

"I am way past the age where being in love means walking while holding hands, going to see a romantic movie together, enjoying delightful candle light dinner at some surprisingly expensive restaurant or nighttime boat ride ---------- but for Ellias, these are the only things that comprises love."

"But Bor....." Nakul had barely opened his mouth to speak when Bornali stopped him by saying, "Please let me finish Nakul."

Nakul was cut off and Bornali continued.

"For me, it's either a serious relationship or no relationship. I can't be in a fling right now."

"Yes, if I become his girlfriend now, he would be more than happy. But eventually, due to our mismatched mentality, we will break up and do you know what will happen next? It will ruin our friendship too. I just don't want to enter into some new relationship by gambling our existing relationship. That's why I am asking if you could just talk him out."

There was a stunned silence between the two. Bornali was looking at Nakul for an answer and Nakul was deciding his dilemma. Finally Nakul said, "Ok, I will talk to him but I don't know if he would listen."

"That no one can tell. But please, at least, talk to him" said Bornali finally relaxed that Nakul would keep her request.

After a small pause he said, "But I still think that he genuinely loves you."

“Please Nakul. Just lay it off. I just don’t want to talk about it” said Bornali in a topic ending tone.

“Sorry” said Nakul and then both of them didn’t speak to one another for the next few seconds. For a fraction of second, Nakul thought that he saw tears in Bornali’s eyes but before he could have been sure of his observation, Bornali walked up to bring the bottle of water from the kitchen.

Nakul decided to remain silent.

After drinking water and resuming her previous position, she broke the ice by saying, “By the way, I was wondering as to why were you reading a book on banking?” indicating by her eye movement the book that Nakul had been reading until Bornali’s entry and was now kept on the tool adjacent to the sofa.

Nakul was at first bold out by this sudden out of track question and then replied, “O yes. Actually I was thinking of appearing for a Banking examination.”

“Why?” asked Bornali the obvious.

Nakul answered, “It’s been three years since I graduated college and though the Malpani case has given me a lot of fame, but I don’t think that fame will help me when I will need food to quench my hunger or medicines to heal my wounds. So I was thinking of having some kind of steady source of income. That’s why banking.”

After a small pause, Nakul said, “Moreover, frankly speaking, I don’t want to take any more financial help from the unknown helper.”

“That’s really mature” said Bornali with an impressive smile.

“Thanks” smiled Nakul, expressing his gratitude.

“See, that’s what I was talking about. Even you have the maturity which Ellias doesn’t” said Bornali suddenly.

"I thought you didn't want to talk about Ellias" interjected Nakul shrewdly with a smile.

"I never said that I did not want to talk about Ellias. I just said that I did not want to talk about Ellias's *infatuation* about me" said Bornali seriously and shutting Nakul up.

CHAPTER TWO

DRESSING SENSE

It's been an hour since Bornali arrived at Nakul's place. They always have their evening snacks together and were now waiting for their third musketeer Ellias to arrive. But they didn't have to wait long.

The door opened and both of them knew who it was. Yet they were surprised. Though it was their friend Ellias, still it wasn't the Ellias they knew.

He was wearing a black coat over his tight formal shirt which was tucked inside his formal pants with a blue scarf rounded against his neck. His hands were covered with black leather gloves with a white round watch tied around his wrist. His head was covered with a round hat and was wearing boots as his footwear.

Both Bornali and Nakul kept looking at him in a state of awe.

Ellias closed the door and while walking towards them asked in an absolutely casual manner with a creepy smile spreading across his lips and dancing his eyebrows, "So, how do I look?"

Both Nakul and Bornali were in too much shock to answer that question.

Ellias took off his hat and keeping it on the table, took his seat on the sofa in between Nakul and Bornali.

"Well, you know, just thought to opt for a style change" he said looking at Bornali and then turning his face towards Nakul asked him the question which Nakul was really afraid to answer honestly, "So, how am I looking buddy?"

"Well, you look absolutely....." Nakul began nervously and as he said the first four words, his brain started revolving with adjectives which Ellias won't be pleased to hear.

"Different" ended Nakul with uncertainty.

"Different? As in good different or bad different?" asked Ellias suspiciously.

"Differently different" said Bornali from his side and Nakul was saved to answer.

Ellias turned towards Bornali with a frown and before he could have asked her a question, Bornali asked him, "But what *motivated* you to opt for a style change all of a sudden?"

Ellias answered lazily, "Well, you know, since we are now a professional investigator of crime, our attire should say so, isn't it? So, when I was choosing my attire, I was thinking as to who is the biggest crime investigator ever and we all know the answer to that question, isn't it?"

"But you know that Sherlock Holmes is fictional, right?" asked Nakul sarcastically.

"So what if he is fictional?" asked Ellias turning towards Nakul and continued, "His crime detection techniques are used in solving real life crimes even today."

"But this attire might have cost you a lot, isn't it?" asked Bornali.

"Well, it was a bit pricy but somehow I managed it" said Ellias without looking into her blue eyes.

"How much?" she asked, targeting straight at Ellias and Nakul also looked eagerly at Ellias.

“Well, Rs. 17000 rounded off” he answered without looking at either of them and playing with his fingers.

“ARE YOU CRAZY?” shouted Nakul and Bornali’s mouth wide opened on Ellias’s stupidity.

Ellias quickly turned towards Nakul and tried to justify his stupidity. He said, “Well, it’s not that crazy. I will be putting it to good use. I will be wearing it every day.”

“That’s even crazier” shouted Nakul at a higher decibel and continued after standing up, “This is not London Ellias. This is Kolkata. And if you think that wearing this attire every day in this hot and humid weather of Kolkata is not crazy, then believe me, you are crazy.”

“Hey, you don’t have to be so mean about it buddy” said Ellias, looking genuinely sad. Ellias’s sad countenance made Nakul feel bad about losing his temper on Ellias’s stupidity.

“I am sorry Ellias but by wearing this attire, you are not only torturing your health but you are also making a fool out of yourself in front of everyone” said Nakul thinking that it would compensate for his loss of temper but the last part of the sentence upset him even more.

When Bornali noticed that they were just making the situation worse, she said to Nakul, “Hey Nakul ! Why don’t you just go to the kitchen and prepare the snacks and I will be arranging the table by then?”

Nakul understood that it was an indication from Bornali to give them a moment and he readily got up and went to the kitchen feeling guilty about Ellias.

Both Ellias and Bornali sat there still for a moment and then it was Ellias who said, “I really thought that you guys will like my new attire.” He mouthed the sentence in a very helpless and powerless manner taking the gloves out of his sweaty hands and throwing them on the table. Bornali felt sympathetic for him.

Bornali after taking a deep breathe said, “Look Ellias, it’s not about your attire. It’s just that we like you the way you are. At least *I* like you the way you are.”

Ellias quickly glanced at Bornali after the last sentence but then quickly took his eyes off her.

Bornali continued, “If you change, you might be better or worse than what you are now. But it won’t be you and nothing in the entire universe is worse than losing yourself. I just want you to be YOU with the same old ratio of perfections and imperfections since the day I have known you.”

There was a small silence for a moment. When Bornali noticed that Ellias won’t be saying anything, she continued, “Moreover an investigator is not known by his dressing sense but by his logic and techniques with which he solves crime, isn’t it?”

“Well, maybe someday books will be written on you about how you solved crimes using your logic and techniques and maybe after reading that book, future crime investigators will try to dress up like you” said Bornali without any hint of smile, though she felt funny inside.

“Yeah right” Ellias gave a sarcastic laugh and then said, “I really don’t care if books are written on me or what impact I have on future crime investigators, but if you like me in the normal way I am, I will be that.”

Though it was an absolutely cliché line, Bornali still gave a slight curving of her lips in the form of a sweet smile. Ellias also smiled.

In the meantime, Nakul came from the kitchen carrying a plate of snacks and Bornali noticing that quickly got up and cleared the table off, while Nakul stood there holding the plate.

Nakul said, still holding the plate in his hand, "Listen buddy. I am really sorry for being so harsh on you."

"No buddy. You were absolutely correct. I was so much drowned in the fame of sudden success that I was trying to change myself into someone else. But now I realize that *people* like me the way I am with my crude ratio of perfections and imperfections" said Ellias.

Nakul had no difficulty in understanding who this *people* is who likes Ellias the way he is. Nakul put the plate on the table while Bornali helped him with the process. Ellias walked towards the basin to wash his hands before eating the food.

"By the way, while I was coming over here, I came across Inspector Sunirmol Ghoshal. He invited the three of us to dinner tomorrow" said Ellias, while applying soap over his wet hands.

"Dinner at Sunirmol Babu's place tomorrow. Why?" questioned Nakul the obvious.

Ellias said casually, "He said that he wanted to discuss some complicated murder mystery that has been the latest hot cake of current criminal investigation."

An intelligent smile spread across Nakul's and Bornali's lips.

CHAPTER THREE

INVITATION TO A CASE

After having the delicious dinner at Inspector Ghoshal's place, Nakul, Ellias and Bornali were now sitting on a comfortable couch while Inspector Ghoshal sat on the adjacent chair carrying a File bearing the number F256.

Ellias, to Nakul and Bornali's gladness, had resumed to his normal attire of T shirt and jeans and he was looking really handsome with his freshly developed biceps.

Inspector Ghoshal had just narrated a brief general description of the mysterious murder case of Mrs. Laxmi Devi and now various thoughts were spurring in the trio's brains.

After a moment of stunned hiatus, it was Ellias who posed the first question. He asked, "Your file says '*Mrs*' Laxmi Devi, but you didn't mention anything about her husband in your narration. Why?"

"That's because, her husband went missing 8 years ago and was therefore put into 'Presumed Dead Category' this year. Though we know his name, but we didn't consider it important enough to put it into the case details as we assume it of no importance in here" said Inspector Ghoshal.

"Pardon me sir, but assumption is a dangerous bad habit. It limits our thinking process" said Nakul with no hint of disrespect.

"Yeah, that's true" said Inspector Ghoshal with a smile towards Nakul knowing that he cannot counter this justification.

"Didn't she have any children?" asked Bornali.

"Well, she had a son but he died ten years ago in a train accident" said Inspector Ghoshal in an instant.

"Who else lived with her in her house?" questioned Ellias.

The answer was "No one. She lived all alone."

"Then who found her dead body and informed the police?" questioned Nakul the obvious.

"Well, it was Hari, who used to shop her the daily essentials" said Inspector Ghoshal and then continued, "We interrogated Hari and he said that he used to get everyday's shopping list a day before along with the money. That Sunday, when he came to deliver the essentials, he found the door unlocked unlike other days. He entered and saw bloodied dragged marks all over the house. On tracking the blood marks, he reached the kitchen, where he saw Laxmi Devi's burnt dead face still burning in the gas flame."

The trio did not utter a word for the next few moments, though each of the trio's facial expressions reflected disgust on hearing the brutality of the attack. Then it was Bornali, who said, "Mr. Ghoshal, would you mind, if we could take the file with us?"

An intelligent smile appeared across the Inspector's face. He said, "I knew this demand will come up. So, I already made a copy of it. You can have this."

By saying this, he extended the file towards her but before she could take it, he said, "But remember, it's confidential. So, respect the confidentiality."

"Don't worry, we will" she said taking the file off his hand with a smart smile.

"We were just wondering if we could talk to Hari once" said Nakul still merged in his thoughts.

"Why only Hari? You should and you must talk to her sister and her family also who are the closest and only known living relatives of Mrs. Laxmi Devi, the details of whom you will find in the file" said Inspector Ghoshal.

"That would be great" said Ellias thankfully.

"Here's an idea. Why don't you guys take a day to go through the file and then meet them day after tomorrow?" said Inspector Ghoshal.

"Yeah. That sounds feasible" said Nakul.

"Then it's final. Come to my place day after tomorrow around 9 A.M. and we will go together for interrogation" said the Inspector getting up from his chair as a gesture of politely requesting them to leave now.

The trio also got up understanding the gesture and seeking his permission left after shaking hands.

Just before, they could cross the threshold of the house, Inspector Ghoshal said, "I hope that you succeed in solving the case. Because if you fail the second time, the credit of your first success goes to luck."

Nakul smiled and answered, "We will try our level best sir but it's an undeniable truth that luck plays a critical factor in every aspect of our life."

After coming out of Inspector Ghoshal's place, the three of them were walking on a footpath towards the local bus stand. It was then when Nakul suggested, "Why don't you guys stay at my place tonight? We can read through the file together and can have a detailed discussion about the case?"

"I don't have a problem staying at your place" said Ellias but Bornali said instantaneously, "But I do."

Both Nakul and Ellias knew that due to some unknown reason Bornali's father never liked them. At times, they have thought that the reason might be the huge difference in their financial backgrounds but neither of them has ever disclosed their thoughts to Bornali.

Hence Ellias asked earnestly, "O come on! Can't you manage your father for once, *beer*?"

"It's not about that Ellias" she said and then continued speaking while walking, "I just don't think that he will see my staying with two boys at night in a very good way and you cannot blame a girl's father for that."

"Yeah right ! Because you are doing it for the first time" said Ellias sarcastically.

"The time I stayed with you guys at night was when my dad went to Scotland for the business acquisition, remember?" she said looking at Ellias.

When Ellias and Nakul did not say anything, she said, "Look guys, I am really sorry. I promise, I will come down really early tomorrow. But please don't waste the night guys. Kindly go through the file carefully and when I come tomorrow, update me with the details." By saying this, she handed the file to Ellias, who took it from her unwillingly.

Finally bidding Ellias and Nakul bye, she boarded the AC bus to her home. Nakul started walking but he had to stop to see Ellias, who was standing and carefully looking at the bus until it took a left and disappeared from sight.

Seeing Ellias, Nakul just thought in his mind, "May be, Bornali is wrong. May be, it is not just an infatuation. At least I hope so."

CHAPTER FOUR

DETAILS IN THE CASE FILE

It's been an hour since Nakul and Ellias had arrived at Nakul's place. Bornali had already whatsapped the two of them fifteen minutes ago that she had reached home safely. Nakul replied with "Ok. We too" while Ellias replied it with "Ok. Take rest and come down early tomorrow."

Bornali replied both of them with an equal pair of thumbs ups. Ellias kept on looking at his phone, until Bornali was online and finally when Bornali went offline, Ellias kept the phone by his side and started reading the case file of Mrs. Laxmi Devi which Nakul was already going through.

The details of the case were as follows: -

Mrs. Laxmi Devi was 64 and lived alone in her house. Her husband Mr. Anshuman Bhattacharya disappeared 8 years ago and was therefore according to the law was put into the Presumed Dead category.

Her son Subhojit Bhattacharya died 10 years ago in a train accident.

Hari is a 25 year old boy who used to shop the daily necessities and deliver to her house. He had been working for her for 8 years and was the first one to decipher her dead body and inform the police. According to the police case file, he is the prime suspect.

The nearest and the only connected relatives of Mrs. Laxmi Devi was her sister Suhasini Chatterjee and her family.

Suhasini Chatterjee was 59 years old and lived with her two sons Nishikant Chatterjee(26) and Ashish Chatterjee(22). Their house is situated at a walking distance of 15 minutes from Mrs. Laxmi Devi's house. They were also informed of the attack by Hari.

The will of Mrs. Laxmi Devi was also found by the police and according to the will, all of the property, money and assets of Mr. Laxmi Devi will be donated to charity.

No life insurance policy was found in her name.

After finishing reading the case details, Nakul said, "Could you see how careless Sunirmol Babu is?"

"How's that?" asked Ellias still merged with the various information in the case details.

"He said that they did not consider it important enough to note down the name of Mrs. Laxmi Devi's husband into the case details but the second sentence only clearly states that her husband's name is Mr. Anshuman Bhattacharya" said Nakul and continued after a small pause, "This clearly proves that he didn't even go through these few lines in the case details also properly."

"What more can you expect from a government servant?" asked Ellias, with a small sarcastic smile.

Nakul also replied him with an exhale of sarcasm.

After a small pause, Ellias asked, "Don't you think it's a bit weird that in the year, her missing husband gets a place in the Presumed Dead Category, she gets brutally murdered in her own house?"

"It's too soon to form any theories" said Nakul, with wrinkled forehead and continued, "Except for one."

Ellias looked at him for the answer to which Nakul replied, “At least her will confirms the fact that the murder is not for property, money or her assets.”

“I don’t think that we can say that either” begun Ellias and then continued his justification by saying, “Unless we know that the will the police found was the only will she ever made.”

After a small break, he said, “If she had made a previous will and changed it to the one the police found, then the beneficiary of the first will has a pretty good reason to kill her on account of personal revenge and the brutality by which the murder has been committed, clearly suggests personal revenge.”

“Hmm” exclaimed Nakul, still merged in the various thoughts that were travelling in the form of waves in his brain.

There went a small pause as both of them were merged in their individual thoughts regarding the jumbled murder case of Mrs. Laxmi Devi. After a small pause, Ellias asked looking at Nakul, “So, how do we start?”

“I think we should start with the basic interrogation of all the names in the files and then analyzing their behaviors and stories, we should decide our next step” said Nakul.

“Agreed” said Ellias and that was it for the two of them that night.

Nakul slept in his room while Ellias, as usual, slept on the couch, in which, according to him, he feels more comfortable than the bed.

The next day was quite normal for them. Bornali, as promised, came down really early and they updated her with the case details. Nakul however noticed something strange.

Ellias remained quite busy in his mobile chatting with someone on Facebook and on being asked, he dodged it by changing the topic.

Bornali also noticed it but did not pay any attention to that as she was busy digesting and analyzing the various case details. Finally she also agreed with Nakul's strategy of basic interrogation.

On the next day, they along with Inspector Sunirmol Ghoshal, went to 64/4S, Boxwall Avenue, which was the address of the victim's sister Suhasini Chatterjee.

Inspector Ghoshal went and rang the calling bell and it was a boy of mid-twenties, who opened the door.

The boy was at first startled on seeing the Inspector but hid his feelings by avoiding to directly look at his eyes.

"Is everyone in there?" the Inspector questioned him in a strong voice.

The boy replied with a polite but nervous nod and a very slight sound of "Hmm."

"Good" the Inspector said and then turning towards the trio said, "Well, he is Hari."

"The one who first found the dead body of Mrs. Laxmi Devi?" questioned Bornali instantly.

"Yes" replied the Inspector and then turning towards Hari, he said, "And, they are my friends and are a part of this investigation. They have some questions for you and you will to the best of your knowledge answer them with absolute honesty."

Hari walked his eyes from the trio to the Inspector and nodded again at his command.

"All yours" said the Inspector to the trio with a smile.

"Well Hari, how did you come in contact with Mrs. Laxmi Devi?" asked Nakul first.

"Well, Suhasini madam recommended me to her sister eight years ago" Hari answered in a polite voice.

"And how did you come in contact with Suhasini madam?" asked Ellias.

"I have been living here since birth" he said.

"What do you mean?" asked Nakul.

"I mean my father was a driver to Suhasini madam's father in law. When he died in an accident, my mother was pregnant with me. Suhasini madam and her late husband Shyamol babu were kind enough to let my mother stay in this house. They were even kind enough to pay for the delivery of my mother but the doctors were unable to save her."

After a small pause, he continued, "They however kept me with them and brought me up. When I was 5 years old, Suhasini madam told me as to what happened to my parents and since then, I have been living here."

The trio thought for a moment and then it was Bornali who asked him, "What work do you do in the house?"

"The usual household stuff like cooking, cleaning the rooms, washing the clothes, shopping the daily essentials, etc.," replied Hari.

"And Suhasini madam recommended you to Mrs. Laxmi Devi for the same kind of household works you do here?" asked Nakul.

"No. She just wanted someone to shop the daily essentials for her" said Hari instantly.

Again there was a moment's silence as the trio was busy in framing questions in their individual minds. Ellias was the quickest and therefore posed the question, "Can you paint us a word picture as to how you came across the dead body of Mrs. Laxmi Devi?"

Hari gave a small exhale of breathe and then thinking slightly he begun, "I brought her the daily essentials as per the list she handed me the day before with the money. But when I reached the front door, unlike the other days, I found it unlocked."

"So instead of ringing the calling bell like every other day, I just pushed the door open and there I saw on the floor blood marks all over. I....."

"Sorry for interrupting" interrupted Bornali and asked, "How were the blood marks? I mean, were they in some particular pattern?"

"I don't remember madam. I was too much scared stiff by the visual" said Hari.

"Please try to remember Hari. It is important" said Bornali trying to pressurize his memory.

Hari said with wrinkled forehead, "I suppose it depicted as if the murderer had dragged Laxmi Devi throughout the hall."

Ok. Then?" asked Bornali.

"Well, one of the blood tracks went into the kitchen and as I followed it to the kitchen, I saw Laxmi madam's face put into the burning flame of gas" he said now breathing heavily.

"You say that one of the blood tracks went into the kitchen. What about the other blood tracks?" asked Bornali.

Hari thought for a while and then answered nervously and unsurely, "As far as I remember, there were only two other blood tracks. One towards the bedroom and one towards the study room but both of these tracks stopped a little ahead of the room entrance."

"And I suppose that the bedroom, study room and the kitchen are one after another, isn't it?" asked Bornali.

"Yes. But how do you know that?" asked Hari astonishingly.

"Well, that's not important" said Bornali and both Nakul and Ellias gave a suspicious look towards her.

Bornali however ignored that and said to Hari with a formal smile, "Well, thank you Hari for cooperating with us. For the time being, we don't have any more questions for you. But if necessity arises, we shall disturb you again."

"So, shall we proceed?" asked Sunirmol babu.

"Gladly" said Bornali with a smile and Sunirmol babu walked ahead into the house followed by the trio.

When they had walked past into the house, Hari finally heaved a sigh of relief.

CHAPTER FIVE

THE INTERROGATION

PART 1

The audience to the first room that Sunirmol babu took them was a middle aged lady. The lady was introduced as Suhasini Chatterjee, the victim's sister.

Sunirmol babu introduced the trio to her in the same manner as he introduced them to Hari with the only exception that there was a tone of sympathy in here. Suhasini however remained absolutely apathetic to the trio's introduction.

None of the trio knew as to how to begun. Yet they knew that if they do not start the conversation, the silence shall continue. So, it was Ellias who broke the ice by saying, "We really can't imagine as to how difficult this time must be for you. But unless you cooperate, we can't be of any help to you."

Suhasini Chatterjee remained static in her position and her swollen eyes remained fixed on the ground. But they were pretty sure of the fact that she had heard him.

When they saw that she remained statue, Nakul unwillingly played his personal experience card. He came forward and said, "My name is Nakul and on the occasion of my tenth birthday, when I returned from my school, I found my parents murdered under mysterious circumstances."

Suhasini Chatterjee's eyeballs shifted slightly from the ground to Nakul's chest. Nakul however continued calmly in his same apathetic tone.

"Till today, I don't know who did that to them or why. But since then, not a moment passes; I don't feel a mixture of emotions of hatred, anger, helplessness and pain. I just don't want anyone else to experience the same."

Suhasini Chatterjee finally opened her mouth after a small silence and it was a question that came out of hers. She asked calmly looking straight at Nakul's eyes, "What makes you think that you can find out the murderer of my sister when you can't even find out the murderer of your own parents?"

Before Bornali could have said anything, Nakul answered, "Because your sister is neither of my parents and so I will analyze the facts of the case with logics and techniques and not by emotions."

"Moreover, frankly speaking, I don't even care if I find out the murderer of your sister or not and maybe it's this carefree attitude that would aid me to unmask the culprit because the more you care about something; the more are the chances that you will lose it like I lost my parents."

By the expression on Suhasini Chatterjee's face, Ellias, Bornali and Sunirmol babu was convinced that Nakul had prepared her at least for her preliminary interrogation.

So, without wasting any more time, Bornali said, "So, if you could kindly answer our questions, it would be of great help in the process of investigation."

Suhasini Chatterjee closed her eyes and opening them turned towards Bornali asked tiredly, "What do you want to ask me?"

"Anything that you wish to tell us that according to you can aid us in the process of investigation" said Bornali kindly and earnestly.

She said after a large exhale of breathe, "Well, I have already told this to the police but still......"

Before she could have continued further, Sunirmol babu cut her words and interjected, "They are not members of the police. They are doing this investigation not out of the compulsion of their duty but out of their own free will. So, start afresh, if you will."

Suhasini Chatterjee gave a look towards the inspector and then looking at Bornali continued, "Well, she was my elder sister but that was only by blood relation. Otherwise, she had been a father, a mother, a friend, a philosopher and a guide to me."

"Our parents passed away in a flight crash when I was 4 years old. But I never missed them as Laxmi di took care of me more as a daughter than as a sister. She even gave me away in my marriage. Even when Shyamol, my husband, passed away in cholera, she supported me and my two sons not only financially but also physically and psychologically."

"Frankly speaking, I couldn't even believe Hari unless I saw her in the police morgue" and after that she started sobbing.

There was a moment's pause and then it was Bornali who asked her, "Mrs. Chatterjee, would you mind telling us your source of finance?"

"I am sorry?" she asked in confusion, still rubbing the tears off her eyes.

"The source of your income from which you run your family" cleared Bornali her question for her.

"Well, it's my husband's pension" she said.

“And is that sufficient for you to run the family?” Bornali asked in a very innocent manner.

“Well, in the present condition of burning price rise, it’s a bit tight. But somehow I try to manage it” she said.

“Do you know that your sister had made a will before her death?” Bornali asked her in a manner as if she doesn’t know it.

Mrs. Chatterjee gave her a sharp look and answered shrewdly, “I know that and I am also aware of the fact that according to the will, all her property, money and assets will be donated to charity.”

Bornali was agile enough to attack her with a counter question by asking, “Then I am pretty sure of the fact that you are also aware that if she hadn’t made a will, then according to law, all her property, money and assets will accrue to you as you are her only and closest living relative, isn’t it?”

“What are you indicating?” she asked angrily.

Bornali replied with absolute calmness, “I am not indicating anything mam. I am just saying that if I had been in your place, I would be pretty angry on her. If I had an elder sister, whom I considered to be my father, mother, friend, philosopher and guide, donates her assets to charity in spite of my poor financial condition, I would be pretty much angry on her.”

“And the brutality with which the murder has been committed clearly suggests enormous rage and hatred” added Nakul.

Mrs. Chatterjee kept looking at the trio with calm angry eyes and then asked in an ice cold voice after a small gap, “Do you wish to ask me anything else?”

“Nothing unless you wish to tell us anything more” Bornali answered for the trio.

"Thank you" Mrs. Chatterjee replied in the same ice cold voice and then turned her face on to the other side.

PART 2

After coming out of her room into the hallway, Sunirmol babu showed them to the room of Mrs. Chatterjee's elder son Nishikant's room. From the outside, it seemed to be like any other normal room but its interior had the strangest peculiar features that the trio had ever seen in their life.

All over its walls were painted and pasted pictures of the strangest forms of art that they had ever come across and in the center of the room over the dirty floor was sitting Nishikant playing with a beautiful Barbie doll.

The artistic pictures comprised of the various torture techniques from ancient, medieval and modern ages which included mutilation, sawing, roasting, disfigurement and so on and what seemed to be playing with a doll from the outside of the room turned out to be a pretty gruesome activity when observed closely.

Nishikant was actually pushing a needle into the left eye of the doll to take it out and from his facial expression; it seemed as if he was enjoying the activity.

As soon as he noticed three strangers into his room, he looked at them and giving a nice innocent smile like a baby greeted them with a very sweet voice saying, "Hello!" Sunirmol babu did not enter into the room as he had a call in his mobile and decided to walk out of the house and have the conversation.

The trio was in too much shock by the view to answer to Nishikant's greeting. Bornali was looking at the disfigured Barbie doll in disbelief and Nakul and Ellias was still looking at the walls in sheer astonishment.

"Excuse me!" Nishikant said in a slightly high voice to draw the trio's attention.

Though the trio heard him, they were still in too much of awe. Bornali was however the first one to resume to her senses and she first opened her mouth by looking into Nishikant's big brown eyes, "Well, we are investigating the mysterious murder of your aunt Mrs. Laxmi Devi and in that respect, we have some questions for you."

Nishikant did not give any answer but just taking the needle out of the left eye of the doll, pushed it into its right eye.

All the three of the trio noticed it but pretended to ignore it. Bornali posed him the first question by asking, "How was your relation with your aunt Mrs. Laxmi Devi?"

"Family relationships are by compulsion and I am not a masochist" Nishikant replied with a smile.

The trio was a bit bold out by the answer. However Nakul voiced looking at him, "Judging by the interior of your room and the present condition of your doll, it seems that you like death by torture, isn't it?"

"O yeah, I love it" Nishikant said with a joyous glow spreading all over his face and then continued, "In fact, my favorite hangout is the chicken shop in the local market. When the butcher beheads the bird and fountain of blood comes out of its severed neck and the bird makes futile efforts of survival till it succumbs to death, I feel a mental peace inside me. I just love it."

The trio was amazed on hearing the explicit description of brutality and how much he adores it. In fact, Nishikant got so much carried away, he continued with absolute excitement, "In fact, in my childhood, I used to pick up house ants and tear its legs one after another or slice it into two with a scissor. It was my favorite past time. In fact...."

Ellias however stopped him harshly and asked, "We are not interested in your childhood. We are interested to know as to where have you been during the time of the murder?"

"Poor trick dude" he said with a laugh and then continued, "I do not know the time of the murder and hence I will not be able to say as to where I have been during that time."

"Then tell us as to where have you been during the entire Sunday?" asked Nakul with gritted teeth trying to control his anger within.

"Well, I was in the house the whole time" he said with a smile, which seemed sweet at first to the trio but now appears disgusting and vomit inducing.

"Do you have any alibi?" asked Ellias sharply.

"I am sorry but I don't have CCTV's installed in my room" he said and again started playing with the doll which included taking the right eye out of the doll and twisting the neck of the doll.

The trio kept looking at him in a manner trying to judge him but he paid attention to neither of them. He, in his own jolly mood, continued torturing the doll.

There was a small pause which concluded when Nakul said, on behalf of the trio, before leaving the room, "We will catch the murderer and once we do, mercy will not be granted on mental condition. Just remember that."

Nishikant just kept looking at them with a smile while his hands separated the head of the doll from its body. Just before the trio could exit the room, Nishikant voiced poetry to them without looking towards any of them:-

The world will rot and will continue to bleed,
No matter how many prayers people plead.
We can't see what today's world we have made,
By the time of realization, we shall all be dead.

PART 3

After exiting from Nishikant's room, the trio remained standing in the hall room silently for a few moments. They didn't talk to each other but were just whirling in their own thoughts. Finally Nakul voiced the words which all the three of them were thinking at that point of time.

"It was like suffocation in there" said Nakul, heaving a sigh of relief.

"I don't care if he is the murderer of his aunt but I would love to see the sadist punk chained on the other side of the prison getting tortured every moment" said Ellias with disgust.

"Let's just talk with Ashish and get over with this interrogation" said Bornali and walked towards the last room, which they were pretty sure of the room of Mrs. Suhasini Chatterjee's younger son Ashish's.

The door was wide opened and from the outside, the trio could clearly see that Ashish was busy playing some game in the computer. From Ellias's love for computer games, it was no difficulty for him to say that it was Call of Duty, United Offensive pack.

"Cool game, isn't it?" voiced Ellias, loud enough for Ashish to hear.

Ashish was so much merged in the game that he was a bit startled on suddenly seeing three strangers inside his room. He turned his face towards the computer to pause the game and then turning towards them asked them their introduction and what they have been doing in his room.

"We have been investigating the murder of your aunt Mrs. Laxmi Devi" said Nakul, on behalf of all the three of them.

"Are you from police?" asked Ashish nervously.

"No. We are private investigators" replied Bornali.

"Private investigators!" Ashish exclaimed with a tone of interrogation and then asked, "You mean like Sherlock Holmes with Dr. Watson and Irene Adler?"

"Thanks for the compliment" said Ellias with a proud smile.

"It wasn't. It was a question" Ashish said in an indifferent way.

Ellias's proud smile burst like a soap bubble while Nakul answered introducing their individual names to him, "More like Nakul Dey, Ellias Khan and Bornali Ray."

"Well, nice meeting you but how can I help you?" asked Ashish after the basic formality.

"By answering our few routine questions that we are about to ask you now" said Nakul.

Ashish wrinkled his forehead and looked towards Nakul but it was Ellias, who posed him the first question.

"How was your relation with your aunt Mrs. Laxmi Devi?" asked Ellias.

"Well, as is my relation with any other stranger" said Ashish confidently.

"Would you mind explaining?" asked Bornali clearly indicating that it was more of a command than a question.

"I barely knew her" said Ashish and then continued after a small breath, "I never went to her house and she never visited ours."

"But your mother said that after your father's demise, your aunt took care of her not only financially, but also physically and psychologically" said Nakul and then concluded by inferencing, "And that's not possible, unless she visited this house. So, it means that either you or your mother is lying, isn't it?"

"Neither of us is lying because when my father passed away, I was just a year old. So, even if my aunt visited this house at that point of time, I don't remember that" said Ashish and then continued, "But since I have gained senses, I do not remember her visiting this house."

"But from the talks we had with your mother it seems that she was pretty close to your aunt. How is it then possible that a person, so close to your mother, never visited this house since you were a year old?" asked Ellias.

"Well, may be, my mother was more close to her than she was to mother because my mother visited her house at least three days a week and my aunt, as I told you, never put her feet in this house to my recollection" said Ashish.

"You say that your mother visited your aunt's house at least three days a week. So, were they any particular three days of the week?" asked Bornali.

"No. It was totally random. Moreover, it was not always even three days. It could have been four, five, and anything" said Ashish and then continued, "Well I just said three days a week to indicate the frequency of her visit to Aunt Laxmi's house. I didn't mean it mathematically."

"Ok. Was her visit on any particular time?" asked Nakul.

"Nothing as such but it was normally after lunch" answered Ashish.

The trio takes in the various information and then it was Ellias who asks him, "You say that your mother visited your aunt quite frequently. Do you know of any particular reason as to why she visited her so frequently?"

"Well, before I answer that may I ask you a simple question?" asked Ashish with a hint of nervousness in his voice.

"Go on" said Nakul.

"Why don't you ask the questions related to my mother to my mother only?" asked Ashish.

Nakul smiles and replies, “Not that it’s any of your business but we came to know of her frequent visits to your aunt’s place from you. So, the questions actually never arose in front of your mother.”

Before Ashish could have said anything, Bornali said strictly professionally, “Well, of course, the facts that you say now will be verified from your mother and I hope, for your own good, they don’t contradict.”

The warning was sufficient to frighten Ashish even more. He gulped and looked at the trio. Bearing a professional formal smile in her face, Bornali questioned, “So, now would you mind us answering as to if you have any idea of your mother’s frequent visits to your aunt’s place.”

“I can’t say for sure but I think it was for general talks because as far as I know, my mother didn’t have any friends and my aunt was the only human being in the planet to whom she can open her heart” said Ashish in a single breathe.

“Ok cool. Now tell me as to where have you been during Sunday?” asked Ellias.

Ashish then gave a small thought and said, “Well, I went to my friend Abhishek’s place the night before on Saturday for our group study for our upcoming examinations. We studied there the whole night and then went to bed at almost 4A.M. in the morning. It was around 11A.M. when I got a call from my mother on my mobile where she was crying and asking me to come home at the earliest possible instant.”

“At that point of time, I didn’t know as to what happened and that tensed me even more. So I quickly freshened myself up and by 11:30 A.M., I was here.”

The trio listened to Ashish calmly and then Bornali said, “Kindly give us Abhishek’s number.”

Ashish's countenance was a sufficient proof of the fact that he didn't expect that. However, quickly resuming to his previous expression he said, "Surely mam. But I do not have his number saved in my mobile as my mobile had a virus attack a few days ago and as I was formatting it, all the contacts got deleted. I had it written somewhere over here but I do not recollect at this very instant. So, if you be kind enough to leave me your contact, I shall whatsapp you as soon as I find his number."

"Sorry, but I can't do that because that might give you the chance to manipulate him" said Bornali and then continued, "because it might happen that after we leave, you might call him and tell him to tell us what you want us to know and then give us his number. So either you give us his number right now or if you fail to do so then you are now taking us to his place. The choice is yours."

Ashish looked sharply at Bornali's eyes and then said calmly, "My aunt died almost a week ago. Wouldn't I have already manipulated him if I had wanted to?"

Bornali smiled and said, "May be but we are willing to take that risk."

Ashish kept looking at her eyes and then lowering his eyes and taking a deep breathe, he said, "I want to say something but only if it doesn't reach my mother's ears."

"You are not in any position to negotiate buddy" said Nakul.

"I am not. I am just requesting and that's also because of the fact that it has nothing to do with my aunt's murder" said Ashish.

"We are listening" said Ellias.

"I wasn't at Abhishek's place the night before. Rather I was with a girl" said Ashish and then looked at the trio's eyes. There was nothing but interrogative calmness in their eyes. Ashish was relieved that they were not at least judging him.

He continued, "Her name is Srijita and she lives just opposite to this house."

"We have been in a relationship for almost a month but neither did she spoke of our relationship to her parents and nor did I tell my mother anything about us. In front of everyone else, we pretend as if we are nothing more than neighbors."

"That weekend her parents went out of her town to visit her maternal grandmother and she wanted to give the chance of physical intimacy to our relationship. I also agreed to her. But I, of course, cannot tell that to my mother. So I lied to her that I was going to my friend Abhishek's place for a study night."

The trio listened calmly to him and then it was Ellias who said, "But still to believe you, we need a confirmation from Srijita and unless she confirms that you were with her the entire Saturday night and half of Sunday's morning, we can't believe you."

"I don't think that's possible because now her parents are back and she would obviously deny the truth to hide our relationship and to pretend that we are nothing but neighbors" said Ashish, now looking nervous.

"Then you are brutally screwed, pal" said Ellias with a sarcastic smile.

Ashish gulped a throat and looked pale in nervousness. The trio felt as if he wanted to say something to them but no words came out of his voice.

"Show us Srijita's number on your mobile!" said Bornali after a moment's hiatus.

Ashish was at first startled and then unlocking his smartphone, going into contacts, showed Srijita's number to them. The trio noticed that Srijita's number is saved as 'Jit" in his contacts. On asking, he said, "Well, I did it intentionally so that if anyone sees her calling, they would think that it is some male friend of mine and hence no suspicion will arise and as a result the secrecy of our relationship remains safe."

"It's for the same reason, on her phone; my name is saved as 'Ash'."

However, Nakul said, "Ok. We will now go and talk with Srijita but you stay here with one of us to avoid the possibility of you manipulating her while we reach her."

Ellias volunteered to stay instantly and both Nakul and Bornali knew as to why he did so. They knew how much Ellias loves computer games more than anything else and by the time, Nakul and Bornali interrogates Srijita, he could play one or two missions of Call of Duty, United Offensive Pack. However Nakul and Bornali did not say anything but left to interrogate Srijita leaving Ellias to stay in Ashish's room.

Nakul and Bornali were about to ring the calling bell of Srijita's house when the door opened and it was a girl of mid-twenties who opened the door. It was Srijita.

"We have been investigating the murder of Suhasini Chatterjee's elder sister and in that respect we have some questions for you" said Bornali introducing them.

"Why am I being questioned?" she asked confusingly.

"Because you are Suhasini Chatterjee's youngest son's girlfriend, who is one of the suspects in this heinous crime of homicide" said Nakul.

"Girlfriend?" she questioned in a manner as if she has never heard of the word before and then continued, "Who said I am Ashish's girlfriend?"

"Ashish" Nakul gave a one word answer.

Srijita looked startled and then said, "Well, he must be kidding or worse lying."

"So you are saying that he didn't spend the night with you last Saturday, right?" asked Bornali.

"No. Of course not" she acted confidently.

"May I see your mobile, please?" asked Bornali suddenly.

"Why?" she asked tensely.

"It was neither a question nor a request" she said strictly.

With trembling hands, she extended her mobile towards her. Bornali took it from her and going into contacts, typed Ashish's name. The phone showed 'No Results Found."

"It seems that you do not have Ashish's number" said Bornali, still looking at the various contacts in her phone.

"Why would I have his number? I told you that he is not my boyfriend" said Srijita defensively.

Bornali however could not resist herself from laughing and said, "Well, you have almost 300 contacts in here. I don't think that all of them are your boyfriends."

Nakul also laughed but Srijita did not find it funny and hence remained stony and pale. However Bornali showed her the contact saved as 'Ash' and asked her as to whose number that is.

All color seemed to draw out of her expression. Still she continued acting. Bearing an artificial smile across her lips, she said, "Well, it's my friend Aishwarya."

Suddenly Bornali pressed the call icon and a call went to the number. Srijita's expression was fade as possible. After two to three rings, Ashish picked up the call and said, "Hello!"

Bornali put the phone on loudspeaker mode and now all the three of them could hear Ashish saying "Hello". Bornali looked at Srijita with a confident smile while Srijita was trembling at that point of time and was unable to look into either Nakul or Bornali's eyes. However Bornali disconnected the call but before that she gave Ashish the confirmation that nothing is wrong with Srijita and they were just interrogating her and it was just a confirmation call to ensure that it was really Ashish's number.

After disconnecting the call, Bornali said to Srijita in a sarcastic manner, "It seems that your friend Aishwarya has a pretty manly voice and it matches with the voice of your neighbor Ashish's."

Managing a smile on her face with a great effort, she said, "Please don't misjudge me but I totally forgot that it was Ashish's number. I saved it as Ash. Actually we met at a neighbor's gathering and from there only, we exchanged numbers but it was purely formal. We never contacted each other after that. You can check our call list or whatsapp."

"It's not difficult to delete a number from the call list or delete an entire whatsapp chat" said Nakul instantly.

Finally Bornali said after a large exhale of breathe, "Since you have decided not to cooperate us with the truth, we do not have any other option than to confiscate your mobile and then retrieve the original call list and whatsapp chat of you and Ashish from the phone company or the cyber department of the police force and then show it to your parents to compel you to tell the truth."

Nakul was confident that it was the final blow and that proved to be true within 5 seconds.

She came closer and held Bornali's arms and pleaded in a whispering tone, "Mam! I am ready to answer anything to the best of my knowledge but can it please not reach my parents' ears?"

Bornali did not answer her question but just asked her once more that if Ashish was with her on last Saturday and when did he leave.

She answered the first question with positive confirmation while the latter was answered loosely stating that she didn't remember exactly the time but it was somewhat after 11.

"Was he with you the whole night?" asked Nakul.

"Yes" she replied nodding her head.

"How can you say that?" asked Bornali.

"Well, as far as I remember, we slept around 3A.M. and at that point of time, he was with me and in the morning, when he woke me up, my head was rested upon his chest. He said that he had a call from his mother asking him to come home at the earliest possible instant. So he left the bed, went to the bathroom, freshened up and left the room. After that I again decided to take a nap but before that my eyes fell on the wall clock and it was showing 11:25 or something."

Bornali eyed her suspiciously and then decided not to ask any more questions to her. She and Nakul were about to depart when Srijita came closer and said in a whispering tone pleading to them, "Please mam. Do not let the news of my relationship with Ashish reach anyone's ears."

Bornali looked at her sympathetically and said, "Don't worry. But I just want to say to you that you cannot hide forever. So it's wise to get out by yourself before someone else finds you out."

With that advice, Nakul and Bornali left. Nakul just called Ellias in his phone to meet them at his place but before leaving confirm Ashish's statement with his mother Mrs. Suhasini Chatterjee.

CHAPTER SIX

OUT OF THE BLUE

Ellias arrived within 15 minutes of the arrival of his two friends. He came and laid flat over the sofa on whose extreme left Bornali was sitting and rested his hairy head over her lap.

"Hey! I am not a pillow" she said irritably.

"Yeah. But I feel comfortable" he said now closing his eyes in pleasure.

"But I don't" she said and removing Ellias's head from her lap, left the sofa and took her seat on the chair adjacent to Nakul.

Ellias however remained on the sofa with the only exception that he now opened his eyes and stared blankly at the ceiling.

Few moments of peaceful silences prevailed till the time Nakul said, "So, inferences?"

Ellias got up and sat straight on the sofa and said, "Well, as per our interrogation, Mrs. Suhasini Chatterjee and her elder son Nishikant have reasons, the reason for the former being sheer revenge of getting cut out of her sister's will while the latter's reason being the satisfaction of his sadist mentality."

"I don't think it is Suhasini Chatterjee" said Bornali, still merged in the various thoughts of the jumbled case.

"Just because she is a woman" taunted Ellias.

"No" she said throwing a serious look towards Ellias and then continued, "Do you remember that while I was interrogating Hari, he said that when he entered the house, he saw there three blood tracks one of which entered the kitchen and the other two stopped a little before bedroom and study room?"

"And you said that the bedroom, study room and the kitchen are one after another, right?" asked Nakul.

"Exactly!" she said and then said looking towards Nakul, "The killer must have dragged Mrs. Laxmi Devi throughout the house to take her to the kitchen but the killer didn't knew from the outside which room the kitchen is. So at first the killer dragged her to the study room but that didn't turn out to be the kitchen. So he tried his luck with the next room which turned out to be the bedroom and finally in his next attempt, he was successful in locating the kitchen. That's why I think that the blood tracks stopped a little before her study room and her bedroom but went straight inside the kitchen."

"That seems possible" said Nakul, listening to her theory with due concentration.

"And if that is, then it is not possible that Suhasini Chatterjee committed the murder because she, as per Ashish, visited Laxmi Devi's house at least three days a week and hence must be well acquainted with the position of the kitchen" said Bornali.

Nakul and Ellias listened to her intently and both of them were impressed by Bornali's theory. However they did not say anything to her.

Bornali continued, "However, if she hired someone else to murder her sister, then it's an entirely different issue."

The theory that appeared to be brilliant to Nakul and Ellias a few seconds ago suddenly seemed diluted and loose by her comment. But still they remained quiet. However Nakul said, "But I do not think that Suhasini Chatterjee could have hired someone to murder her sister because I don't think that she could afford the finance required to pay someone just to take revenge. After all, her source of income is only her husband's pension, isn't it?"

"And I don't think that Nishikant is either the murderer" continued Nakul.

Ellias asked in a depressed deportment, "Why?"

"Because he is a sadist since childhood. Then why would he suddenly murder his aunt?" asked Nakul.

"There is always a first time for everybody. For some, it's early and for some, it's a bit late" said Ellias, trying to prove Nishikant guilty.

"Even if that be accepted, then tell me why he would project his sadistic mentality in front of us, being fully aware of the fact that it could divert our attention towards him?" asked Nakul.

"May be, he is pulling the old trick of lying with the truth" said Ellias and then continued, "May be he is trying to blind us not with the dark but with excessive light."

Nakul and Bornali remained quiet and whirled in their individual thoughts. After a few moments, Bornali asks, "So, what about Ashish?"

Nakul had barely opened his mouth to speak when Ellias interrupted him by saying, "Before that, may I say something, out of the track?"

"That you always do. So why take permission this time?" asked Bornali satirically.

Ellias ignored her sarcasm and said, "I really find the couple, I mean this Ashish and Srijita, very cute and adorable. I mean, the way, they were trying to protect the secrecy of their relationship with their futile lies was really sweet, isn't it?"

"Yeah, totally diabetic" said Bornali sarcastically.

"O come on! You can't be that unromantic" exclaimed Ellias.

"Yes I am if you perceive the concept of romance only from cliché movies and third grade novels" said Bornali in a rude manner.

Seeing the situation getting hotter, Nakul asked to no one in particular, "Can we return to track please?"

"Well, he is the first one to divert" said Bornali in a low tone.

"And you followed him" said Nakul loud enough for the other two to hear and then without giving her any opportunity to speak further said, "So, let's just cut the crap and focus on the case."

"Sure" said Bornali and that was it.

They were analyzing the various aspects of the case when suddenly Nakul's phone rang. It was Mr. Sunirmol babu on the other side.

"Is there any progress on the case?" he asked.

"Well nothing significant until now" replied Nakul.

"Then I think that I might be of some help to you in this regard" he said and then when he noticed that Nakul waited for him to continue further, he said, "There is a woman who claims to be the daughter in law of Mrs. Laxmi Devi."

Nakul's investigative intuition told him that it's crucial and important to the case and hence without wasting any time, the trio started for the police station and in half an hour, they were there.

"She claims to be the widow of the Late Subhojit Bhattacharya, the late son of the victim Laxmi Devi. She even showed us a valid marriage registration certificate of her with Laxmi Devi's son" said the Inspector.

"You can't call that a claim if the marriage registration certificate is valid. It's a fact then" said Nakul.

"But what is she doing here?" asked Bornali.

"She claims the property of Mrs. Laxmi Devi to her nine year old son Anish, he being the victim's first and only blood" said the Inspector.

"That means she doesn't know about Mrs. Laxmi Devi's will, donating all her assets to charity, isn't it?" asked Ellias.

Before the Inspector could have parted his lips to answer, Bornali said, "Either that or she pretends to not know that or she doesn't know that the police found the will."

The Inspector just nodded his head in affirmation. There went a moment of silence and then it was Nakul who said, "Would you mind if we talk with her?"

"I would if you don't" said the Inspector and then asked his subordinate to send the lady inside his chamber.

The lady entered the room with her nine year old son and took her seat on the empty chair as ordered by the Inspector. The trio was introduced to her as the Inspector's friends and a part of the investigative team while the trio learned that the lady's name was Manjira Kyn.

"How did you come to know of Mrs. Laxmi Devi's murder?" was the first question that was posed to her and Ellias was the one to ask her that.

"It's all over the news" she replied calmly.

"But why are you here? It's been ten years since your husband died and you kept no connections with your mother in law whatsoever and now after her mysterious murder, you are suddenly here, claiming her property and assets to your son. Why?" asked Bornali.

"Because I have no emotional attachment to her. But her property and assets is the rightful legal claim of my son and that's why I am here" she replied with absolute confidence and perfect calmness.

"Unfortunately you are wrong Ms. Kyn or shall I say Mrs. Manjira Bhattacharya, depending on your 'valid' marriage registration certificate that you brought with yourself" said Nakul and then continued, "Because prior to your mother in law's death, she had made a will in which she donated all her property and assets to charity."

Her jaws dropped and shock was prevalent in the awe of her expression. She had not come prepared for this. Unconsciously her lips parted and the words came out in a voice of hatred, "That cranky bloody bitch."

"I beg your pardon" said Nakul on behalf of all of them.

She didn't answer but just said, "That means I came all this way for nothing" and was about to get up from the seat and leave with her son when Bornali said, "We have some questions for you."

She looked at Bornali rudely, did not say anything but just resumed her position on the seat.

"We would prefer to interrogate you alone and believe me it's for your own honor and dignity" said Bornali and the subordinate was called by the Inspector to take her son out into the waiting room.

"What is your source of income?" asked Bornali.

"I sing in a dance bar" she replied cold bloodedly.

"And what do you mean when you say that you sing in a dance bar?" asked Bornali in a professional manner.

She gave a nasty smile and then said with gritted teeth, "You bloody well know what does that mean." A small gap for inhale of oxygen and then she said, "It means that I am an escort and my pimp arranges high range clients for me in exchange for a percentage of my share of income."

There goes a momentary silence and then it was Bornali who continued, "I think that I can safely presume that you are not escorting out of your own free will and financial crisis seems to be the only reason to have compelled you to enter this profession. Now getting your mother in law's property could easily absolve your financial crisis and could safely secure the future of you and your son. So it is a possible theory that you went to your mother in law's house, asked for her financial help and her on refusing to help you, you killed her in sheer anger."

"That's a wonderful theory mam but you should know that I have been escorting for 8 years. So tell me as to why I would be waiting for 8 years to kill her?" she asked, trying her best to suppress her anger within.

"Because prostitution is possibly the only profession in the world where the pay scale diminishes with age and you might have started realizing the crude fact that your days are nearing an end in your profession and so to secure the future of your son, you might have gone to your mother in law seeking her help" said Bornali quickly.

"You seem to know an awful lot of stuff about prostitution. Are you also in the same profession?" asked Manjira, finally pouring her venom out.

"Don't you dare bitch" said Ellias aggressively, trying to defend Bornali's honor.

But Bornali stopped him by saying looking at Manjira with calm eyes, "Relax Ellias. Truth hurts the most, isn't it?"

Manjira didn't answer and there went a moment of stunned hiatus. However it was Bornali who broke the silence by saying, "We need to speak to your pimp and so I would request you to kindly call him and get him down here at the earliest possible instant."

"What does he have to do with this case?" she asked her rudely.

"We don't have the need to answer your questions" said Nakul.

"And neither do I have the compulsion to answer yours" she said.

"As a matter of fact you do have the compulsion to answer our each and every question. You are a suspect in this crime and unless you want to spend the next few nights in jail before you get prosecuted in front of the court, not only for prostitution but also for murder, you will do exactly as we say" warned Ellias to her.

Manjira took out her mobile phone from her jeans and made a call and after disconnecting the call, she said, "He will be here in less than an hour."

Manjira, along with her son, was sitting in the waiting room of the police station while BEN was inside the private chamber of Inspector Sunirmol Babu. They were waiting for the pimp to arrive when it was Nakul who voiced out, "Guys! I just remembered something."

"Remember when we were interrogating Hari, he said that his father died in a car accident and his mother died while giving him birth" asked Nakul.

"And when he was five years old, he came to know of it from Mrs. Suhasini Chatterjee" supported Bornali.

"Exactly! But that is Suhasini Chatterjee's version of Hari's parents' death that was fed by her to Hari. What if that is not true?" asked Nakul.

"What do you mean?" asked Ellias, being confused as to where Nakul was heading with this.

"I mean that do you really think that there is so much goodness in Mrs. Suhasini Chatterjee that in the era of burning price rise where her only source of income is her husband's pension, she would bring up her driver's son?" asked Nakul.

Ellias and Bornali didn't answer but still Nakul continued. He said, "May be Mrs. Suhasini Chatterjee's version is false and the truth is something else and may be the truth is in some way or the other linked with the mysterious murder of Mrs. Laxmi Devi."

"But dude, we need to place our trust on some basic axioms. Otherwise we cannot proceed in the case" Ellias pointed out the basic point.

Nakul was about to answer when the door of the chamber opened and the subordinate officer walked in and said, "The pimp is here. His name is Sourav."

"Send him in and only him" ordered the Inspector.

A man came in nervously. He had curly hairs and was thin as a stick. His body complexion was fair and his height reached almost 5ft. His eyes were blue in color and his lips had turned black, may be due to his excessive smoking.

The man quickly rounded his eyes throughout the room and then it was Inspector Sunirmol babu who ordered him in his strong voice to take a seat in one of the empty chairs.

He sat and then it was Nakul who first asked him, "Coming straight to the point, how long have you been arranging clients for Manjira?"

"What happened sir? Is there something wrong?" he asked fretfully.

"Nothing happened and nothing is wrong but there will be if you don't answer our questions honestly and properly" said Ellias from Nakul's side.

He gulped a throat and then answered stuttering, "Since 8 years."

"How did you come in contact with her?" asked Bornali.

"I and her family lived in the same slum and..." he had barely begun to speak when Bornali interrupted him by asking, "What do you mean by her family?"

"I mean her and her mother. Since the time I have known her, she lived with her mother. I had never seen her father. Her mother was a maid servant and she used to study in the local government school. But when her mother died due to wrong treatment in tuberculosis, she quit her school and started working as a full time maid servant in the houses in which her mother used to work."

"It must have been a year and a half since then when she brought a man home and they started living together in her room. On asking, I came to know that the man was her husband."

"What was the man's name?" asked Nakul.

"I used to call him Subho da but as far as I remember, his full name was Subhojit something" said Sourav unsurely.

The trio understood that the man was none other than Subhojit Bhattacharya, the son of Mrs. Laxmi Devi and was confirmed by Sourav's statement that Manjira was truly wedded to Laxmi Devi's son Subhojit Bhattacharya. They became pretty sure of the fact that Manjira was not lying about her marriage with Subhojit Bhattacharya. However they did not say anything to Sourav about what was going on in their minds.

"Go on" said Ellias.

"They had a kid in the first year of their marriage and things remained in her favor for another year. Frankly speaking, I had never seen her happier ever. Her marriage and her child birth seemed to put a glow in her face and her life."

"But when her husband's mutilated body was found near the railway tracks, she was devastated for obvious reasons.

She had already left her job as maid servants in the houses to take care of her new born baby and their only source of income was her husband's job as an accountant in the local ration shop. But when her husband passed away, she broke, not only emotionally but also financially."

"She tried to get into her previous jobs but she faced nothing but rejections or at least she said so to me. So, one day, she came to me and said that she wants to work for me knowing fully the type of work I do. I even asked her as to if she is sure about her decision and warned her that once she is scarred, she is scarred for life. But she said that she had thought this through. She said that she wants to give her son the life he deserves even at the cost of ruining her own."

"So I decided to help her and since then she has been escorting for me" Sourav completed.

"You didn't help her. You just used her disadvantage to your advantage" said Bornali coldly.

"Yes mam but isn't that how every profession in the world works?" asked Sourav.

Bornali didn't answer but just said after a small gap, "We require the name of all the clients Manjira has served in the last two months. Can you provide us with that?"

"Surely mam! It's right here in my mobile" said Sourav and then took a mobile out of his pocket.

He opened a folder named "Employees" and inside it there were various sub folders. He clicked on the sub folder named "Manjira Kyn" and inside it, he clicked on the excel file named "Accounts."

The file was opened and he handed the phone over to Bornali. She saw that a table has been made with the headings "Client name", "Date" and "Payment." She scrolled through the data but she couldn't find any familiar names.

Nakul and Ellias also rechecked but the results remained same.

Nakul, Ellias and Bornali had hit a dead end in the case and they had no idea as to how to proceed further. After a moment of stunned silence, it was Ellias who said, "Thank you Sourav for your cooperation. If anything else is required, we shall contact you." Sourav nodded politely and left the room.

Sourav had barely left the room when he reentered quickly and said, "I think I should mention one more thing to you. I do not even know if it is relevant to the case but I think that I should mention that about a week and a half ago, a man came to the bar and enquired about my escort services."

"Why do you think that we should know about that?" asked Nakul.

"Because he didn't come for escort service. He just wanted to know about the life of the escorts like who are they, who are there in their families and so on."

"Who was he?" asked Ellias.

"I don't know. When he first came in, I thought that he was a client and so when he asked me about the escort service, I naturally assumed that he wants to be served. So I started showing him in my mobile the various pictures of my escorts and the type of pleasurable services that they will provide and the costs associated with them."

"But after viewing all the pictures, he said that he didn't want to be served. He said that he is an amateur filmmaker who wants to make a festival oriented documentary on the life of escorts across our nation and in that respect he wants to have a personal interview with the escorts."

"So after a little negotiation which ended in my favor, I gave him the names and addresses of some of my escorts which included Manjira's name but later on when I asked them, I found out that none of them had been visited by anyone for any kind of interview."

The trio and Inspector Sunirmol babu listened to him with due concentration and then it was Bornali who asked him, "Did the man leave you any number or any name?"

"He didn't leave any number. He just said that his name is Sundar Singh."

"Was he a Sikh?" asked Bornali instantly.

"Yes. He was. He had a big yellow turban on his head with a very large beard and a ....." and before Sourav could finish his description of the man, Bornali starts laughing. The others looked at her surprisingly and then she says after a moment, still with a smirk across her face, "Don't you understand? He wore make up."

"Sikh make up is the easiest and the most efficient make up to hide one's true identity and he did exactly the same" said Bornali.

There went a moment of silence after which Bornali said, "Thank you so much Sourav for your cooperation. If anything else is required, we shall contact you."

Sourav finally left and the trio started digging deep into their individual minds as to how they should proceed further to unravel the mysterious murder case.

CHAPTER SEVEN

THE PLAN

The trio was sitting in Nakul's house in absolute silence merged in the labyrinths of the case. They were trying to see the case from various perspectives. Finally it was Bornali who spoke.

"From what we know the only person whom Mrs. Laxmi Devi has wronged is her daughter in law Manjira Kyn. She did not include her in her will as a result of which she was compelled to resort to escort services that would provide her financial support for the sustenance of her and her son."

"Now it might be a possibility that she came to her mother in law Mrs. Laxmi Devi's house, asked for her financial support (for she knew that her days in prostitution are nearing an end), she refused and in sheer anger, she killed Mrs. Laxmi Devi."

"And the way in which the murder has been committed clearly suggests immense hatred and anger" said Nakul.

"Yes. But we do not have any proof as to whether Manjira truly visited Laxmi Devi's house or not and a statement without proof is a statement in vain."

"Now let's assume few things. Firstly, let's assume that Manjira murdered Laxmi Devi. Secondly, let's assume that she hired someone to do it for her and thirdly let's assume that someone did it for her out of his own free will. So no matter what we assume, Manjira seems to be the connection here. Right?"

"Precisely" said Ellias.

"So, here the plan goes" said Bornali and Nakul and Ellias listened to her with due concentration.

"First we take Manjira in our custody and then we gather all the persons involved with this case in one place. We tell them that Manjira is the killer but do not tell them anything more or answer any more of any questions. We also tell them that since she hasn't yet made her confession yet, we will apply third degree torture on her to make her do it and once she does it, then only she will be allowed to meet anyone."

"Now if the killer is among them and he had killed Laxmi Devi for Manjira out of his own free will, he will definitely try to stop that and the only way left to him will be to contact us. But if Manjira is the killer then I am pretty sure that she will spill up the truth in the first few moments of torture. I don't think that she could bear police torture for too long."

"But what if Manjira is not the killer and is in no way connected with the murder?" asked Ellias.

"I have thought that too. If that be the case then the murderer will be glad that we are on the wrong track and won't do anything" said Bornali.

Nakul and Ellias thought the plan for a moment and then it was Nakul who said, "When you say that if the murderer had murdered Mrs. Laxmi Devi for Manjira out of his own free will, then hearing this news, he would try to contact us, what did you mean?"

A grin passed through her face and then she said, "There goes the climax of the plan."

"After speaking with all the persons involved in the case about Manjira, we three won't disperse together. Two of us will go together and one will go separate. Now if the killer is among them then I am pretty sure that the killer will follow the singular one of us and will try to use that person as leverage to free Manjira."

"What if the killer kills the other person?" asked Ellias, now a bit scared.

"He won't because that won't materialize his objective of freeing Manjira. He would only want to use that person as leverage" said Bornali with absolute confidence.

"There seems to be an awful amount of risk in this plan" said Nakul.

"I know that but I do not have a better solution than this and I don't think that you guys have either" said Bornali.

Both Nakul and Ellias knew that she was correct but still they didn't want to go through this plan. It's not just because of the risks associated with it but because the assumptions were too vague and the probability of success also seemed to be too low. Still they knew that they didn't have any better plans than Bornali. So they agreed.

After a moment of pause, Ellias asked, "So, who will bell the cat? Who will be the singular one of us?"

"I think it should be me" said Bornali as a statement.

"Not a chance" said Nakul and Ellias together.

"I know that you guys are worried about me but kindly hear me out."

"People suffer from the misconception that women are weaker than men and that's why women are considered an easier bait than men. Now if the killer is among them and either one of you goes singular then the killer may or may not pursue you but if I go singular then the killer will definitely pursue me because of the world's misconception about strength of women."

It was perfectly logical but Nakul and Ellias were more concerned about the safety of their friend than the perfection of logic.

"But I don't want you to be in danger" said Ellias.

"But do you want to find out the murderer?" asked Bornali.

"Not at the cost of losing you" Ellias answered straightforwardly.

"You won't" said Bornali and then looking towards Nakul she said, "You guys won't."

From the facial expressions of Nakul and Ellias, Bornali became pretty sure that they were more nervous than her and she felt glad that she was blessed with such good friends.

CHAPTER EIGHT

THE REVELATION

Things happened exactly as per the plan. All the people involved with this case were gathered at Suhasini Chatterjee's place and the trio arrived there and said exactly as planned.

Many questions rose and even voice of protests came from Sourav. But the trio answered to none and left. Nakul and Ellias took right towards the latest shopping mall that was inaugurated last week while Bornali took left and walked towards her home as slowly and casually as possible.

Nakul and Ellias walked silently and they didn't speak to each other until they reached the cafeteria of the mall. They took a seat in the food court and were waiting for Bornali's call. Bornali had told them that if nothing happens, she will call them once she reaches home.

Their hearts were beating at the highest possible rates and all forms of negative thoughts were coming in their thoughts. Nakul was biting his nails and Ellias was shaking his legs in sheer nervousness. Almost an hour passed but no call came. Unable to control the nervousness anymore inside, Ellias spelled out, "I think we should make a call to her."

Nakul nodded and Ellias was about to make a call from his mobile when a text message alert came in his mobile and that was from Bornali. It read as follows.

If you can't come to the below mentioned address within half an hour, then don't bother to come at all. I will send her to you, but in pieces.

An address was given. Below it was written....

If you call the police, I will call the morgue, you know, for an advanced booking.

"No time to waste" said Nakul and entering the address on GPS followed its directions. Within 20 minutes, they were in their required destination, panting and sweating.

It was an old abandoned school. 8 years ago, when a communal riot broke out, a group of anti-socials set the building on fire and all the students and teachers who were present there at that point of time were burnt alive. Since then, the school has been kept abandoned and many haunted childhood stories have also cropped up from there.

It was almost 8:45 PM and the building with no electricity was looking as haunted as possible. Nakul and Ellias was also scared but not of ghost but of Bornali's whereabouts.

"I swear to Allah that if something happens to Bornali" Ellias had barely begun with gritted teeth when Nakul stopped him heavily by saying, "Nothing will happen to her. We won't let anything happen to her."

Suddenly another text alert entered Ellias's mobile and it said

Fourth floor, Room no. 35.

The duo ran and reached the fourth floor and started searching for Room no. 35. Nothing was much clear in the darkness but finally Nakul found a room whose door was open and on it was engraved the number 35.

He drew Ellias's attention to it and both of them frantically entered the room. It was complete darkness and hence to find out their third friend, they started shouting her name.

No reply came.

Nakul and Ellias switched on the flashlights of their mobile and started searching for Bornali, shouting her name as loud as possible. Suddenly Ellias's flashlight caught the face of Bornali. She was on a wooden chair near the blackboard, her hands, legs and mouth tied.

Ellias quickly called Nakul and both of them quickly freed her of her bondages. The first thing that came out of her voice was, "Our plan worked!"

Before the duo could have reacted to that, a man entered the room from outside carrying a hurricane in his hand and as Nakul and Ellias put their flashlights on his face, the figure became clear.

It was Ashish Chatterjee, Suhasini Chatterjee's youngest son.

Nakul and Ellias's jaws dropped but Ashish remained calm. He walked forward and said, "Before you come to any conclusion, can you just hear me out?"

They were in too much shock to answer that question and hence they chose silence as their answer. Taking 'yes' for silence, he started speaking, which the trio listened with due concentration.

It was almost a month ago when one day I came home quite late at night. I was at a friend's house party and I was heavily loaded. When I came back home and knocked the door, I thought that Hari will open it for me. But unfortunately my mother was still awake and she opened it for me.

I was being barely able to stand straight. My eyes were red and puffy and I could not even look into her eyes properly. I was embarrassed to a great extent.

I walked past her slowly with my head bowed down and I had walked a maximum of two to three steps when I took a nasty burp and vomited and passed out in the hall. After that I have only scattered memories of she with the help of Hari taking me into the bathroom, taking my clothes off, giving me a bathe in cold water and then throwing me into the cozy comfortable bed of my room.

When I woke up the next morning, I had a bad hangover but after a glass of hot lemon water and a cup of strong coffee, I started feeling better. But as I started feeling better, a feeling of embarrassment and humiliation came crushing down upon me. I could not face my mother.

When she noticed that I did not come down for breakfast, she came up and opened the door of my room. I could not look into her eyes. But instead of shouting at me or slapping me, which at that point of time I thought I deserved, she quietly came and sat beside me.

She took a deep breath and said, "It does not matter if you say sorry to me or not. But I know that you are feeling it right now in your mind and for that I am really proud of you Ashish."

I looked at her but could not make an eye contact. She continued, "You don't need to promise me anything but I just want you to promise yourself that you will never repeat such a thing ever again in your life."

"I have already promised myself that" said I instantly.

Finally the embarrassment and humiliation started abating and I could finally look into her eyes. She gave a kind smile and then she said, "Let me tell you a story" and she started.

"You know, my sister Laxmi di had a son named Subhojit. He was brilliant in academics, well mannered, kind and humble. We all thought that he had a bright future. But all that shattered when he fell in love with the maid servant of his house."

"Manjira, the maid servant worked in my sister's house and GOD knows how Subhojit fell in love with her. When Subhojit said that to Laxmi di, she was furious for obvious reasons. But Subhojit was stubborn. Going against the will of his own mother, he married Manjira and as a result my sister cut her son not only out of her will, but also of her house and life.

My sister didn't even listen to her husband and hence Subhojit left along with Manjira never to return home. After some time, Subhojit's dead body was found in the railway tracks. No one knows what happened to him and how did he die. But we all think that he suffered from depression and hence finally committed suicide. My sister did not even see the dead body of her son as she said that her son died for her the moment he left her for the house's maid servant."

There was a moment's silence and I did not say anything. My mother continued, "He could have been with us right now living a happy and a prosperous life but his one wrong decision changed everything. That is why I am telling you this story because you are also a good person like Subhojit but sometimes good people also make bad choices and then the ramifications are terrible. So I just want to say to you that meet with everyone but don't mix with everyone."

After her advice, she left and I kept sitting where I was.

Since, I did not have my breakfast; I was feeling a bit hungry before the scheduled lunch time. So I went down to have my lunch and as I passed my mother's room, I heard her talking to someone over her mobile. It would not have drawn my attention if I hadn't listened to her exact words, "Of course I haven't told Ashish anything about that." That grew my suspicion.

I knew that if I ask her straightforwardly, she would cleverly dodge it and manipulate me with some lie. So I knew that would have been a failed attempt. But then I suddenly remember that she always records her call and the matter was as simple as anything.

In the evening, when my mother went to the local temple for attending the regular evening veneration, I listened to her recorded call and that changed everything.

The call was of my mother with her sister Laxmi Devi.

After hearing the call, I came to know that Subhojit did not commit suicide. Rather he was murdered and then his body was thrown away in the railway tracks projecting it as suicide and all of that was planned by his own mother for punishing him for the crime of falling in love with the maid servant of the house and marrying her.

Laxmi Devi knew that Manjira was paralyzed with the death of her husband and was resorting to escort services to sustain herself and her son but she didn't help them. She enjoyed their pain and suffering.

From the recorded call, I also came to know the name of the bar where Manjira sings and from where she provides escort services to various clients.

I went to the bar disguised as a Sikh person and a fake name and there I met Sourav, the pimp, who thought me to be a client in need of escorts. He started showing me the pictures of various escorts that included Manjira's picture too.

I knew that if I directly ask about Manjira, then that would arise suspicion in his mind. So I said to him that I am an amateur filmmaker who is on his way on making a festival oriented documentary on escort services in India. He bought that and after a bit of price negotiation, he provided me with a list that contains the names, contacts and addresses of the various escorts. It obviously included Manjira's details. My work was done there. So I thanked him and left.

After that I followed Manjira for quite a while without her notice and saw how terrible her life was. She was escorting day and night and was treated by her client worse than a piece of furniture. But she digests all that humiliation and pain in silence just for the sake of the sustenance of her and her son.

I don't know why but I felt a strong fire of hatred and anger inside me for Laxmi Devi. I never met her or spoke with her or visited her house but I knew deep down inside that I hated her from the very core of my heart. That hatred only gave rise to my plan.

I knew that Srijita was eager to give our relationship a chance of physical intimacy and I also knew that her parents would go out of town for the coming weekend. I knew what I had to do.

I told Srijita that I want to be physically intimate with her and she could not be more thrilled. So I said to her that I will be staying with her on Saturday night and she readily agreed because her parents were out for the weekend. That was the first part of my plan.

I told my mother that I will be staying at my friend Abhishek's house on Saturday night for a study night and she readily believed me without any suspicion.

I took a bottle of whiskey with me to Srijita's place and on asking I told her that I brought it to celebrate our first intercourse with each other. She believed me innocently.

After we had our intercourse, we finished the bottle of whiskey. I pretended to drink while she drank almost 5 pegs. I also mixed some ENO to each of her pegs to increase her intoxication. My intention was to create an alibi with her. I wanted her to remember that I was there with her when she fell asleep and I was also there with her when she woke up. That's how if she gets interrogated, she will say that I was there with her for the whole night and my alibi will be safe. My plan was successful.

After she fell asleep at around 3, I remained awake waiting for the sunrise. It would be around 5:30, when I quietly swooped out of the bed, put my clothes on and walked out of the house. I walked to Laxmi Devi's house and I was lucky enough to find the door unlocked.

From the gap of the door, I could see Laxmi Devi walking all over her house with a plate of fresh flowers, sweets and burning candle spreading the purity of the mixed fragrance to every corner possible. An electricity of anger and hatred passed through my veins. My brains had stopped working and my mind didn't even cross the thought that someone else could have been inside the house.

I walked in, almost pushed by some invisible force, and I killed the sinister beast. From that moment till today, not a moment passed when I felt bad for what I did that day.

However, after that I walked back to Srijita's place, took my clothes off and slept besides her in the same manner in which she last remembered me.

There was a pin drop silence when Ashish finished telling his story to BEN. The trio listened to him with due concentration but could not decide as to what to say to him as all the three of them were going through a stage of moral crisis.

"If you think that what I did was wrong then I will not protect myself" said Ashish breaking the silence.

Still the trio remained silent. They were trying to overcome their dilemma. Finally it was Bornali who asked him, "Whatever wrong Mrs. Laxmi Devi did, it was to her son and her daughter in law and by extend to her grandson, but she didn't do any wrong to you. Then what was your relationship with Manjira that just because Mrs. Laxmi Devi wronged her, you went off to kill her and that also with such brutality?"

Ashish gave a sad smile and said, "It was the same relationship that you have with the conductor of a bus in which you have never rode or your relationship with a shopkeeper from whose shop you have never shopped. I felt the same pain that you feel when you see that in some terrorist attack, innocent children becomes orphan or a newly wedded bride becomes a widow. It was the basic human relationship between two humans. When I saw her in pain, I felt pain that she has been living through this hell just because of Mrs. Laxmi Devi and so when I killed her with that brutality, I felt a mental peace within me. A strange kind of happiness I felt when I saw Laxmi Devi in misery and pain and her horrible death only absolved me of the mental pain of impotent helplessness that I was going through since I have known her ugly truth."

"This lecture on human relationships does not suit in the lips of a murderer" said Ellias shrewdly.

"Who isn't a murderer?" asked Ashish sarcastically and then answered without giving anyone any opportunity to speak any further. He said, "Turn over the pages of history books. The heroes whose names we have studied since our first standard in school are nothing but murderers. Most of the freedom fighters are murderers. Not only are they, even

GODs are murderers too like Durga killing Asur or Rama killing Ravana."

"Do you really compare yourself with GOD and freedom fighters?" asked Nakul with hilarity.

"Not at all because I do not want to be a marketable product in the profitable business of religion and education" he said, suppressing his anger within himself.

"But whatever you did, it really didn't help Manjira, did it?" asked Bornali and then stated, "After all, she is still an escort who is still living through a hell of mental and physical abuse for the sustenance of her and her son."

"I didn't do it for her. I did it for myself and I am glad that I did it" he said without any hint of hesitation and then continued after a small gap, "I will admit that I was scared of getting caught and that's why I created the false alibi with the aid of Srijita but I cannot live with the burden of someone else getting tortured and punished for a crime that she hasn't committed."

"So when you three said that you will torture Manjira to make her confess, I feared that she might succumb to the pressure and once she does, there will be no way out for her. That's why I kidnapped Bornali mam to gather you three together without the company of police and tell you the truth. Now as I have made my confession to you, if you think that I am wrong, then feel free to hand me over to the cops."

Ashish took out Bornali's mobile from his jeans and extending it towards the trio, he said, "I have already switched on the call recorder in your mobile, thereby recording my entire confession. If you decide to hand me over to the cops, this can be of some aid to you. But please don't include Manjira in all these. She has already suffered enough."

Bornali took her mobile and switched off the call recorder. She looked at Ashish and Ashish said, "I have also transferred the recorded call of my mother with Laxmi Devi so that you can verify if I was speaking the truth."

"No need of it and no need of your confession. But we will keep it just for our records" said Bornali calmly keeping the mobile in her jeans.

"You go Ashish and do not speak of this night to anyone. We don't know as to what happened tonight here and neither do you" said Nakul, on behalf of BEN and walked off with his two friends.

CHAPTER NINE

FACING THE FAILURE

On the next day, Nakul, Ellias and Bornali were sitting in the police station with Inspector Sunirmol Babu. The trio said to him that they decided to quit the case as they could find no way to progress any further.

"It seems that in the Malpani case, you just got lucky" said the Inspector, with a hint of tease in his tone.

"I suppose you are correct" said Nakul, acting depressed.

"But it seems that the police hasn't made any progress in the case either" said Ellias with a twitching of his lips.

Inspector Sunirmol babu recognizes sarcasm pretty well. He replied with an absolute formal smile, "Every day, thousands and thousands of cases gets registered in the police file. So the police can't give individual attention to every case. It takes time but you never know. May be we will solve it. Just keep your eyes open on the newspaper."

"Definitely we will" said Bornali with a smile and continued, "And we are really thankful to you for offering us this case. Sorry to disappoint you, but this has been a hell of a ride for us."

After that the trio got up, shook their hands with the Inspector and left his room. They were about to walk out of the police station when they suddenly noticed Mrs. Suhasini Chatterjee with her youngest son Ashish.

Mrs. Suhasini Chatterjee came forward to Nakul and said looking straight into his eyes, "I should have known. When you can't even find out the murderer of your own parents, how could you trace the murderer of my sister?"

Nakul gave a slight look towards Ashish and then looking towards her said with absolute seriousness, "You were right, mam. I was overconfident."

"You might have given up but I won't. One day, I will hunt the bloody murderer down and tear off his flesh to see what rotten dirty blood runs through his veins" she said, trembling in anger.

Nakul didn't know how to respond to that. He just took a deep breathe and said looking towards Ashish, "Take care of your mother" and walked off quietly with his two best friends.

Nakul, Ellias or Bornali did not turn back though all of them were pretty sure that two types of gazes were on their back -------------- one of disappointment and the other of respect.

9 798887 496917

Printed by Libri Plureos GmbH in Hamburg, Germany

Printed by Libri Plureos GmbH in Hamburg, Germany